Now We Have
a Baby

Dear Josie,

You are a
wonderful
big sister.
Love, ♡
Linda

NOW WE HAVE A BABY
Copyright © 2004 by Good Books, Intercourse, PA 17534
This 8" x 8" paperback was first published in 2006.
International Standard Book Number-13: 978-1-56148-553-6
International Standard Book Number-10: 1-56148-553-5
Library of Congress Catalog Card Number: 2004007821

Text by Lois Rock
Illustrations copyright © 2004 Jane Massey

Original edition published in English under the title
Now We Have a Baby by Lion Hudson plc
Copyright © Lion Hudson 2003.
North American edition entitled **Now We Have a Baby** published by Good Books, 2004

Printed and bound in Mexico.

Library of Congress Cataloging-in-Publication Data
Rock, Lois, 1953-
  Now we have a baby / Lois Rock ; illustrated by Jane Massey.
    p. cm.
Summary: A simple introduction to babies and what it is like to be part of a family with a new
baby.
  ISBN 1-56148-553-5 (paperback)
  [1. Babies--Fiction. 2. Family life--Fiction.] I. Massey, Jane, 1967- ill. II. Title.
  PZ7.R5875No 2004
  [E]--dc22   2004007821

Now We Have a Baby

Lois Rock
Illustrated by Jane Massey

Intercourse, PA 17534
800/762-7171
www.GoodBks.com

Here is a baby,
newborn and tiny.
There are lots of
things to know
about babies.

Babies need to sleep a lot. You sometimes have to be **quiet** when a baby is sleeping.

Babies wake up at funny times. When they do, they can be very noisy.

Babies need lots of looking after. Sometimes you will be very busy looking after baby.

Sometimes
a baby has a
lot of fun.

Everybody
seems to love
a baby.

Sometimes
you can feel
left out.

But all tiny babies
are little persons who
need people to love
them.

Love helps them
learn about smiling
and talking.

Love helps them
learn about helping
and playing.

Love helps them learn about caring and sharing.

Love makes a baby
a part of our family,
for a family is love.

Welcome, Baby!